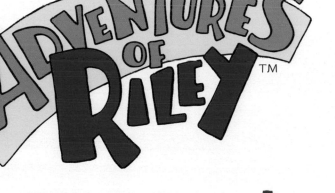

Project Panda

Adventures of Riley ™

Project Panda

JIUZHAIGOU

Dear Riley,
What looks like a black-and-white
teddy bear and is an international
symbol for endangered species?
The giant panda, of course!
Join me, Aunt Martha, and Cousin
Alice as we visit China, the only
place in the world to find wild pandas. We'll be studying how they live
so we can help find a missing panda
at China's famous Wolong (Woo-
long) Panda Reserve. With only
1,600 pandas left in the wild, every
panda counts!
Uncle Max

Riley J. Mitchell

Connecticut

USA

BY

Amanda Lumry

AND

Laura Hurwitz

SCHOLASTIC PRESS ★ NEW YORK

A special thank-you to all the scientists who collaborated on this project. Your time and assistance are very much appreciated.

EaglemonT
Press

All photographs by Amanda Lumry except:
pg. 19 snow leopard © Cyril Ruoso/JH Editorial/Getty Images
pg. 23 dawn redwood © Dr. Jun Wen/Smithsonian Institution

Illustrations and Layouts by Ulkutay & Ulkutay, London WC2E 9RZ
Editing and Digital Compositing by Michael E. Penman
Digital Imaging by Phoenix Color

Library of Congress Control Number: 2006024465

ISBN-13: 978-0-545-06829-1
ISBN-10: 0-545-06829-0

10 9 8 7 6 5 4 3 2 1   08 09 10 11 12

Printed in U.S.A.   08
First Scholastic paperback printing, May 2008

A portion of the proceeds from your purchase of this licensed product supports the stated educational mission of the Smithsonian Institution— "the increase and diffusion of knowledge." The name of the Smithsonian Institution and the sunburst logo are registered trademarks of the Smithsonian Institution and are registered in the U.S. Patent and Trademark Office. www.si.edu

2% of the proceeds from this book will be donated to the Wildlife Conservation Society. http://wcs.org

An average royalty of approximately 3 cents from the sale of each book in the Adventures of Riley series will be received by World Wildlife Fund (WWF) to support their international efforts to protect endangered species and their habitats. ® WWF Registered Trademark Panda Symbol © 1986 WWF. © 1986 Panda symbol WWF-World Wide Fund For Nature (also known as World Wildlife Fund) ® "WWF" is a WWF Registered Trademark © 1986 WWF-Fonds Mondial pour la Nature symbole du panda Marque Déposée du WWF ®
www.worldwildlife.org

A portion of the proceeds from your purchase of this product supports The Wyland Foundation, a 501(c)(3) nonprofit organization founded in 1993 by environmental marine life artist Wyland. By bridging the worlds of art and science, the Wyland Foundation strives to inspire people of all ages to become better stewards of our oceans and global water resources.
http://wylandfoundation.org
www.wyland.com

We try to produce the most beautiful books possible and we are extremely concerned about the impact of our manufacturing process on the forests of the world and the environment as a whole. Accordingly, we made sure that the paper used in this book has been certified as coming from forests that are managed to ensure the protection of the people and wildlife dependent upon them.

Before going to China, Uncle Max took Riley to the National Zoo in Washington, D.C. They watched the pandas munch on giant, leafy stalks.

"Why do they eat so much bamboo?" asked Riley.

"Pandas are mainly **vegetarians**," said Uncle Max. "They used to be meat eaters, but scientists think they switched to plants because they couldn't compete with other **carnivores** for prey. Bamboo is their main food source, but zookeepers will also feed them special biscuits or apples."

"That's like switching from hamburgers to celery," said Riley. "**Permanently!**"

The Great Wall

Beijing

Terra Cotta Figures
Xian, China

The trip to China took two long days and many long flights.

When Uncle Max and Riley finally landed in Beijing (Bay-jing), Aunt Martha and Cousin Alice were there to greet them. Together, they toured downtown Beijing and many more of China's amazing sights.

3

They began their panda research in the Jiuzhaigou (Jo-ji-go) Valley, a nature reserve about 800 miles west of Beijing.

"With all the new bamboo growth around here, it's the perfect place to learn about panda habitat," said Uncle Max. "Pandas are hard to find since they prefer to live high up in the nearby mountains, but sometimes they will wander down for food or warmth. What we learn today should help our panda search at Wolong."

"Oh, no!" Riley shouted. "I think I left my sneakers in Beijing!"

"That's okay," said Alice. "You can borrow my purple ones."

"Purple?" asked Riley. "No, thanks. I think I'll stick with my red sandals." By the time they reached a nearby Tibetan village, Riley's feet were very sore.

"You should try Alice's sneakers," said Aunt Martha. "You might like them!" Riley groaned and put them on.

"Purple is your color," teased Alice. Riley turned as red as his sandals.

5

Walking along a wooden boardwalk, they passed by the most beautiful lakes and waterfalls that they had ever seen.

"No wonder the Chinese call it 'Fairyland on Earth,'" said Aunt Martha. Riley's feet were feeling much better.

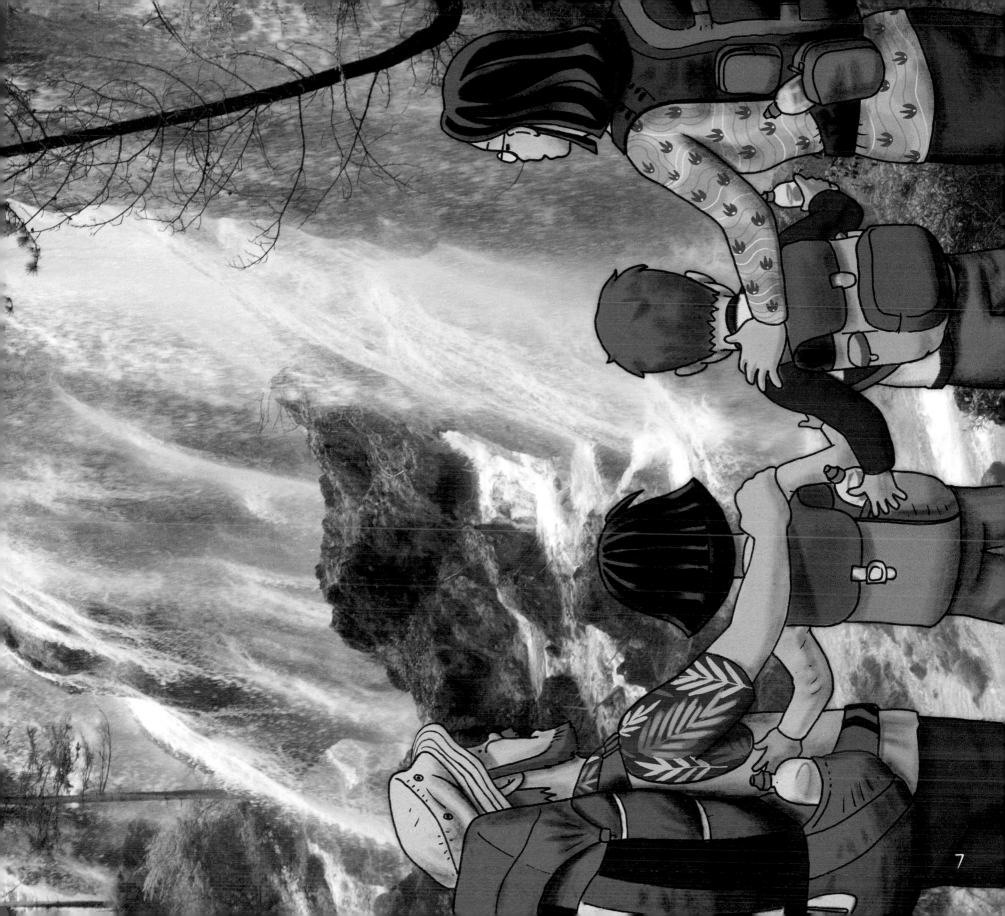

Bamboo

➤ It is actually a species of grass.

➤ There are about 25 different types of bamboo.

➤ It regularly flowers and dies across large areas. This is called synchronized flowering. It can take a year for bamboo to grow back, and 15 or more years to return to full size.

—Colby Loucks, Deputy Director, Conservation Science Program, World Wildlife Fund

Golden Snub-Nosed Monkey

➤ It acts like a **ventriloquist** by making vocal sounds without opening its mouth.

➤ Its major food sources are **lichen** and bark.

➤ It sometimes gathers in groups of up to 600!

—Colleen McCann, Curator of Primates, Wildlife Conservation Society

"Look at all this bamboo!" said Uncle Max. "If only I had Internet access out here, I could ask my fellow scientists what species it is."

"How do pandas eat bamboo?" asked Riley. "It's so hard and tough."

"Pandas have **adapted** over time," said Uncle Max. "Their **molars** have become flat to crush, grind, and eat bamboo. And look at these fresh paw prints and shredded bamboo! There was a panda eating right here earlier today."

"Incredible!" said Aunt Martha. "Even though logging in this area has stopped, it has destroyed much of the pandas' habitat and food supply. It is taking the panda population a long time to recover, since they give birth to only one cub every two to three years, and bamboo takes so many years to grow back."

Riley pulled out his camera, but when he looked through the lens to take a picture, something looked back at him! He jumped backward, knocking Uncle Max's notes everywhere.

"Sorry!" Riley said, as the animal ran off. "What was that?"

"Let's go see," said Uncle Max.

Fujian Cypress

➤ It is native to the wet, tropical climates of China, Vietnam, and Laos.

➤ It is evergreen and can grow up to 114 ft. (35 m) high.

➤ It is used to make furniture, walls, and roofing. It can also be processed to make oil for makeup and medicine.

—Sylvia Stone Orli, Museum Specialist, Department of Botany, National Museum of Natural History, Smithsonian Institution

> It is most closely related **Red Panda** to raccoons, and similar to giant pandas and bears, but is now considered a "family" of its own.

> Also known as the Lesser Panda, it is about the size of a house cat.

> It was discovered in 1821, 48 years before the giant panda.

—Zhiyong Fan, Species Program Director, WWF China Program Office, World Wildlife Fund

Farther down the boardwalk was a little animal chewing on some bamboo.

"Oh, it's just a raccoon," said Alice.

"Look again," said Uncle Max. "It's actually a rare red panda. Even though it's called a panda, it's not closely related to the giant panda. They do have one thing in common, though. See how it holds that branch? Both red pandas and giant pandas have developed a **specialized** wrist bone that acts as a thumb to help them hold bamboo."

Food Preparation

Museum

Hospital

The next day they drove 250 miles southwest to the 500,000-acre Wolong Panda Reserve, the first and largest panda reserve in China. They were given a tour of the research station, where they saw the panda hospital, museum, nursery, playground, and, of course, more pandas than they had seen in their lives.

"It's like an entire zoo full of pandas!" said Alice.

Breeding

Nursery/
Playground

"Normally there are about 80 pandas inside the research center and 150 outside in the natural habitat part of the reserve," said their guide. "But as you know, we're down to 149 in the wild, and we're really starting to get worried. Like most pandas, our missing female lives alone in a **territory** of about 2 square miles. If you find a panda in that area, it'll probably be her."

That night, Riley dreamed he was searching
for pandas in the Chinese forest.

Their panda search began at sunrise. Alice could barely keep her eyes open.

"Riley, you should borrow Alice's sneakers again," said Aunt Martha.

"No problem," said Riley. Wearing purple wasn't that bad, and it sure beat wearing sandals.

"The best part is, I won't need my notebook," said Uncle Max. "Wolong has gone Wi-Fi."

"Why-Fye? Is that Chinese?" asked a sleepy Alice.

"Wi-Fi is short for wireless fidelity," said Uncle Max. "It means I can use my laptop anywhere in the reserve to send e-mails to the research station."

16

In the early morning mist, they drove halfway up a nearby mountain to the missing panda's **territory**.

As they hiked along a narrow pathway, a large antelope crashed through the trees in front of them.

"Look at that takin run!" exclaimed Aunt Martha.

➤ A baby takin has chocolate brown fur, which turns golden yellow as the takin grows older.

➤ A takin will spend the warm summer months in high mountain meadows, and cooler months at lower elevations.

➤ It will stand up on its hind legs and push trees over with its front legs in order to eat from them.

—David Powell, Assistant Curator of Mammals, Wildlife Conservation Society

Takin

18

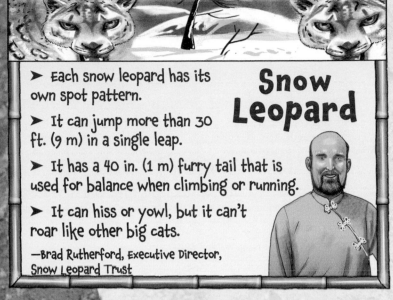

➤ Each snow leopard has its own spot pattern.

➤ It can jump more than 30 ft. (9 m) in a single leap.

➤ It has a 40 in. (1 m) furry tail that is used for balance when climbing or running.

➤ It can hiss or yowl, but it can't roar like other big cats.

—Brad Rutherford, Executive Director, Snow Leopard Trust

Snow Leopard

Suddenly, another animal streaked into view. A beautiful black and white spotted cat paused on the path in front of them, then disappeared after the takin.

"Unbelievable!" said Uncle Max. "That was a snow leopard! No one has ever seen one here before. I should tell the reserve right away. They could . . ."

Uncle Max was interrupted by booming thunder—but there wasn't a cloud in the sky. The rumbling grew louder and louder until the ground began to shake. Alice froze, and Aunt Martha reached for her.

Looking up the mountain, Riley saw a river
of mud and rocks coming directly at them!
"LANDSLIDE!"
He grabbed Uncle Max and Aunt Martha,
pulling them all to safety. The path was
buried behind them.

"Landslides are common around here," said Uncle Max. "Thanks for pulling us out of the way, Carrot Top!"

"Thank Alice's sneakers," said Riley. "I couldn't have done it without them. But how will we get back?"

"Wi-Fi!" said Alice. "We can e-mail Wolong and tell them what happened."

"Brilliant!" said Uncle Max.

Dawn Redwood

➤ It is a conifer, which means it has cones on it, like a pine tree.

➤ It grows quickly and can reach heights of 100 ft. (30.5 m).

➤ It is considered a "living fossil" because it was first found in fossil form, before a live tree was discovered in 1944.

—Dr. Jun Wen, Research Botanist, Smithsonian Institution

With the click of the "send" button, their **SOS** message went out.

http://www.wolonggandareserve.com

SOS!

A landslide has washed away the trail, and now we're trapped on the mountain. Please send help!

—Professor Maxwell Plimpton and Family

23

Minutes later, they got a response: "Stay put—we're on our way."

While waiting for the rescue team, they searched along the pathway for signs of the panda. They found nothing.

"I packed some apples for lunch," said Aunt Martha. She tossed one to Riley, but it landed in the bushes and rolled down the side of the mountain.

"It's okay. I'll get it," said Riley, carefully pushing his way through the thick brush.

His apple had fallen into an oddly shaped hole.

That's not a hole, thought Riley, *that's a footprint—a panda footprint!* There were panda tracks everywhere! He followed them to a patch of half-eaten bamboo. *This can only mean one thing!* Riley said to himself.

26

The branches of a nearby pine tree rustled. Something was up there! Riley looked at his apple and suddenly knew what to do. He set it closer to the tree and backed away. To his delight, a panda climbed down and picked it up. As the panda settled back into the tree, Riley saw something else—something small.

Giant Panda

➤ A giant panda can bleat like a sheep, honk like a goose, chirp like a bird, and bark and growl like a dog!

➤ To help it stay warm in winter, it will eat up to 60 lb. (27.2 kg) of bamboo per day. It does not **hibernate.**

➤ It loves snow and will slide down snowy slopes for fun!

—Lisa Stevens, Curator of Primates and Giant Pandas, Smithsonian Institution

Riley ran back to the others. "I think I've found our missing panda— and she has a baby!"

28

Uncle Max took a digital picture of the mother panda, which Riley e-mailed to the research center. A message quickly came back: "You've found our missing panda! Is she okay?"

Riley grinned and typed back: "Uncle Max says she looks great—and is the mother of a healthy young cub! What a great day!"

Rescuers led them around the landslide, down the mountain, and back to Wolong.

Giant Panda

➤ It is a good swimmer.

➤ It eats mostly bamboo, but will also eat lizards, insects, bird eggs, and meat.

➤ In Chinese, the giant panda is called da xiong mao, which means "big bear cat."

—Karen Baragona,
Yangtze Basin
Program Leader,
World Wildlife Fund

As a reward for their discovery, Riley and Alice got to play with some toddler panda cubs.

"Hopefully, the baby panda we saw today will grow up to be as healthy as these cubs," said Aunt Martha.

"And," said Uncle Max, "since Riley was able to attract the panda with his apple, the scientists here are going to add apples to the rice and vitamin mixture they usually feed the pandas."

"Cool!" said Riley. "Hopefully they'll **adapt** to apples as quickly as I adapted to Alice's purple shoes." He looked at the young pandas sitting all around him. *Every panda counts.*

31

Back home, Riley couldn't wait to get his own pair of purple sneakers. He told everyone about the snow leopard, the landslide, and finding the missing panda—and its new cub. A few days later, a package arrived for him from China: his red sneakers! He returned to living the life of a nine-year-old . . . until he once again got a letter from Uncle Max.

Where will Riley go next?

FURTHER INFORMATION

Glossary

adapt: to change or get used to a place or situation

carnivores: animals that mainly eat meat

hibernate: to sleep through the winter

international: including every country in the world

Wyland 100 Mural Project

Student artists from around the world will join internationally renowned marine life artist Wyland this summer in Beijing, China, for a pre-Olympic art project celebrating our oceans, lakes, rivers, streams, and wetlands. As part of "Hands Across the Ocean," the artists will create hundreds of canvases representing United Nations and Olympic member countries.

The project will be the grand finale of Wyland's 30-year quest to paint 100 giant marine life murals around the world.

lichen: a plant made up of fungus and algae that forms crusty, leafy, or branching growths on rocks and trees

molars: teeth toward the back of the mouth that have flat, broad surfaces for grinding food

permanently: for always

SOS: a call for help

specialized: made to work in a certain way

territory: the area that an animal defends and considers its home

vegetarians: people or animals that do not eat meat

ventriloquist: a performer who talks with little or no lip movement

JOIN US FOR MORE GREAT ADVENTURES!